This book belongs to

....

NO MORE BABIES!

Madeleine Cook   Erika Meza

OXFORD
UNIVERSITY PRESS

Sofia was just finishing her greatest ever tower.

This will be my masterpiece!

When suddenly . . .

... Arlo ruined **everything.**

That was just the start . . .

At lunch, Arlo
started a food fight.

Next he banged a drum,
and would not stop!

Then he slobbered on
Sofia's favourite toy.

When Sofia wanted Mummy
and Daddy to read a story . . .

We're going to need more wipes!

. . . Arlo created a stink.

Sofia was not having a great day.
But surely Mummy and Daddy's news
would cheer her up . . .

'Sofia, you're going to be
a big sister again!'

Sofia looked at
Mummy and Daddy.

Then she looked at Arlo.

PARP!

Then she looked at
Mummy and Daddy again,
and suddenly . . .

'NO MORE

BABIES!'

'Oh,' said Mummy.

'What's the matter?' asked Daddy.

Sofia didn't know
where to begin . . .

'Babies are *messy*,

and *noisy*,

and *smelly*.

Burp!

'They are *snotty*,

A-choo!

and *grumpy*,

Waaaaaaaa!

and *jibbery!*'

Fee-fee!

What does that even mean?

'Babies never say *please* or *thank you*.

They just take your clothes,

and books,

Hey, those
are mine!

and toys . . .

. . . and they steal mummies and daddies, too!'

'Oh dear,' said Mummy,
'I think you'd better tell
us all about it.'

Ah-ah!

So Sofia told Mummy and Daddy
about Arlo smashing her tower,
and throwing his breakfast.

And how it always seemed that Arlo
was taking her Mummy and Daddy, too . . .

They had a cuddle to make everything better.

'Come on,' said Mummy.
'I think we should play a game—just you and me.'

Mummy took Sofia to play football,

while Daddy and Arlo
painted a picture.

Then Daddy and Sofia
re-built her tower,

while Mummy and
Arlo baked cookies.

After that, everyone snuggled up together—
and Arlo showed Sofia the picture he'd painted for her.

Then he did something he'd never done before . . .

'So-fee-ah,' he said.

'Arlo just said my name!'
said Sofia.

'You've got to be kidding me,' said Daddy.

'I'm sure he'll say 'Daddy' soon enough,' said Mummy, with a smile.

After that, things seemed much better.

Arlo is still *messy*,

and *smelly*,

Parp!

and *slobbery* . . .

But Sofia loves him very much.

'Okay, you can have one more baby,' said Sofia,
as Mummy and Daddy took her to bed.

Mummy and Daddy gave each
other a funny look . . .

'How about twins?' said Daddy.

For Freya—M.C.

Para Gus, who had to endure me
as an older sister—E.M.

OXFORD
UNIVERSITY PRESS

Great Clarendon Street, Oxford OX2 6DP
Oxford University Press is a department of the University of Oxford.
It furthers the University's objective of excellence in research, scholarship,
and education by publishing worldwide. Oxford is a registered trade mark
of Oxford University Press in the UK and in certain other countries

Text and Illustrations copyright © Oxford University Press 2020

The moral rights of the author have been asserted

Database right Oxford University Press (maker)

First published in 2020

British Library Cataloguing in Publication Data

Data available

ISBN: 978-0-19-277612-9

1 3 5 7 9 10 8 6 4 2

Printed in China

Paper used in the production of this book is a natural,
recyclable product made from wood grown in sustainable forests.
The manufacturing process conforms to the environmental
regulations of the country of origin.